Dear Parent:

Buckle up! You are about to join your child on a very exciting journey. The destination? Independent reading!

Road to Reading will help you and your child get there. The program offers books at five levels, or Miles, that accompany children from their first attempts at reading to successfully reading on their own. Each Mile is paved with engaging stories and delightful artwork.

Getting Started
For children who know the alphabet and are eager to begin reading
• easy words • fun rhythms • big type • picture clues

Reading With Help
For children who recognize some words and sound out others with help
• short sentences • pattern stories • simple plotlines

Reading On Your Own
For children who are ready to read easy stories by themselves
• longer sentences • more complex plotlines • easy dialogue

First Chapter Books
For children who want to take the plunge into chapter books
• bite-size chapters • short paragraphs • full-color art

Chapter Books
For children who are comfortable reading independently
• longer chapters • occasional black-and-white illustrations

There's no need to hurry through the Miles. Road to Reading is designed without age or grade levels. Children can progress at their own speed, developing confidence and pride in their reading ability no matter what their age or grade.

So sit back and enjoy the ride—every Mile of the way!

To my sweetie, Seamus
C.D.

For my nephew, Daniel
T.L.

With special thanks to Jenny Montague, Assistant Curator of Marine Mammals at the New England Aquarium in Boston, Massachusetts.

Library of Congress Cataloging-in-Publication Data
Daly, Catherine.
Whiskers / by Catherine Daly ; illustrated by Tom Leonard.
p. cm.—(Road to reading. Mile 2)
Summary: Describes how different animals use their whiskers for survival.
ISBN 0-307-46214-5 (GB)—ISBN 0-307-26214-6 (pbk.)
1. Whiskers—Juvenile literature. [1. Whiskers.] I. Leonard, Thomas, ill. II. Title. III. Series.

QL942 .D26 2000
591.47—dc21 99-089175

A GOLDEN BOOK • New York
Golden Books Publishing Company, Inc. New York, New York 10106

ISBN: 0-307-26214-6 (pbk.) A MM
ISBN: 0-307-46214-5 (GB)

Whiskers

by Catherine Daly

illustrated by Tom Leonard

It is night.
A cat is hunting a mouse
in a field of tall grass.

The cat cannot see the mouse.
But he knows where it is.
His whiskers feel the grass
move when the mouse runs by.

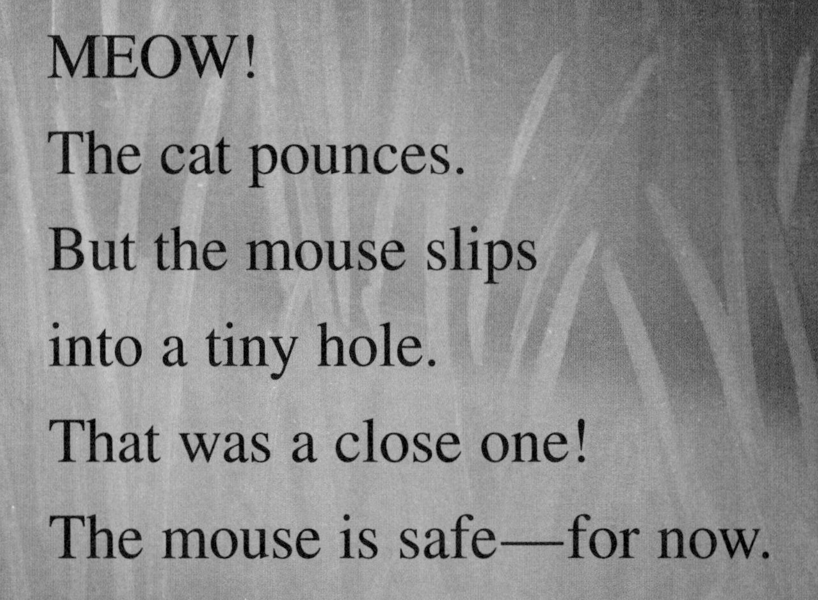

MEOW!

The cat pounces.

But the mouse slips

into a tiny hole.

That was a close one!

The mouse is safe—for now.

How did the mouse know
she could fit into the hole?

Her whiskers told her!
If her whiskers can fit,
so can the rest of her body.

Whiskers are special
hairs that can feel.
They are part of an
animal's sense of touch.

Have you ever played
pin-the-tail-on-the-donkey?
With a blindfold on,
you can't see anything.
So you use your hands
to feel the way.
That's a lot like the way
an animal uses its whiskers!

1
3
4
5
2

Naked mole rats live
in underground tunnels.
They are nearly blind.
But they never get lost.

The whiskers on their heads and backs help them feel which way to go.

These seals swim
under the ice,
where the water is dark.
Their whiskers help them
find holes in the ice
so they can poke out
their heads to breathe.

A seal's whiskers
are also used for hunting.
The whiskers feel
ripples in the water
when a fish swims by.
Then it's dinnertime!

Seals have about forty whiskers.
Walruses have almost 700!
That's more than any other mammal.

Walruses have very sensitive whiskers. They use them to find clams and other food on the ocean floor. Their whiskers work a lot like hands.

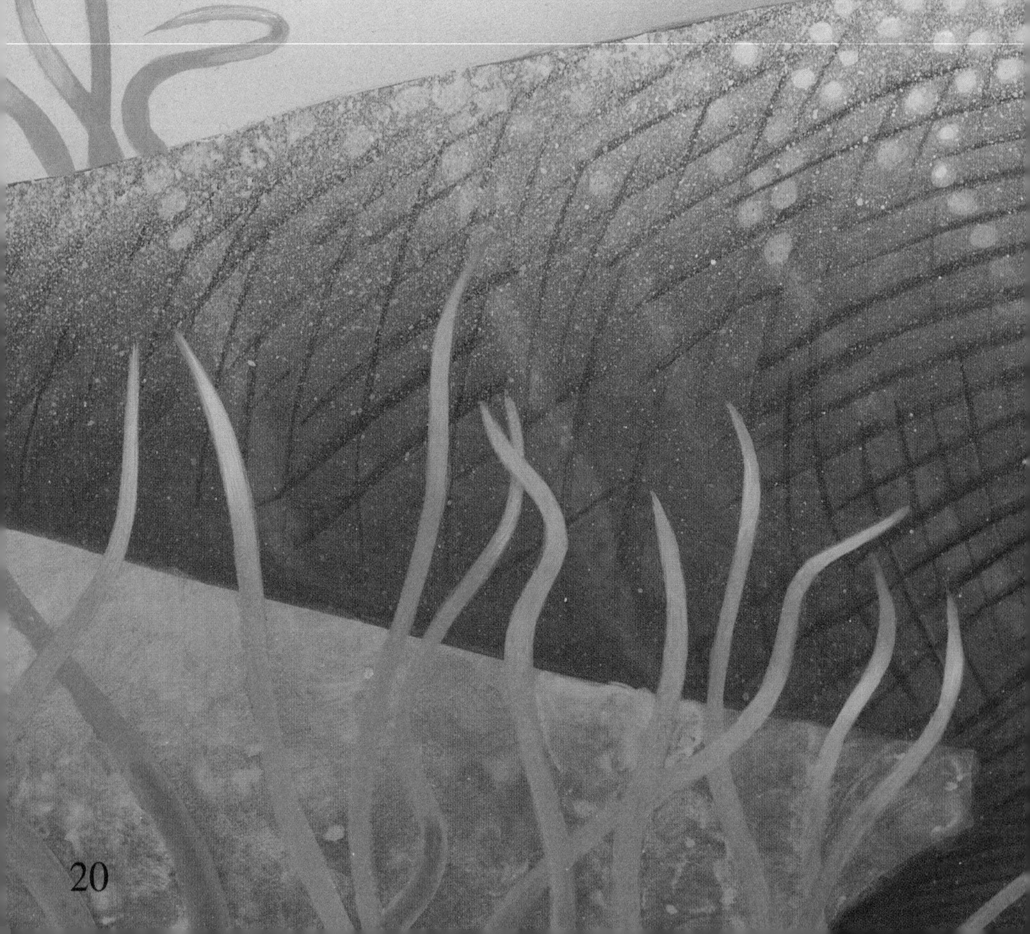

Walruses also use
their whiskers
to show affection.

A mother walrus will often brush her whiskers against her baby.

Have you ever seen a sea lion
balance a ball on his nose?
He was using his whiskers!

The sea lion's whiskers feel
which way the ball is going.
That way, the sea lion knows
which way to move his neck
so the ball won't fall off.

There are some people
who believe that whiskers
have special powers.
They think that
a tiger's whiskers
can cure toothaches,
or give people courage.

Some "whiskers" are not really whiskers at all!

The *barbels* on this catfish are made of skin, not hair.

This porcupine cannot
feel anything with his quills.

Whiskers come in all shapes and sizes, and animals use them in different ways.

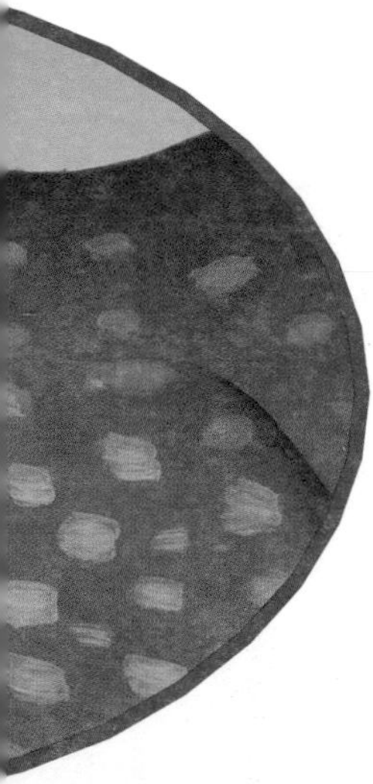

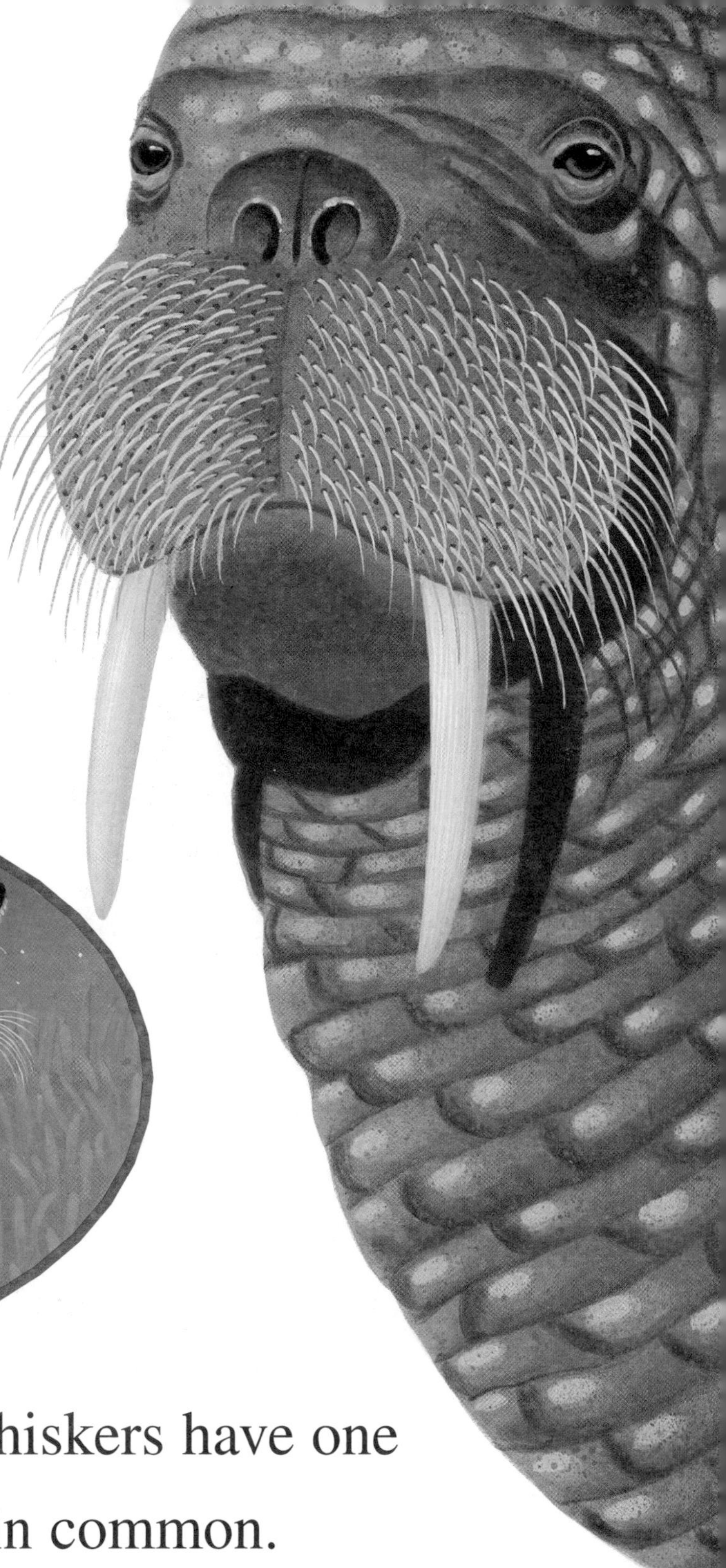

But whiskers have one thing in common.

They help animals survive!